SPACE PENGUINS

GALAXY RACE!

L.A. COURTENAY

ILLUSTRATED BY
JAMES DAVIES

STONE ARCH BOOKS
a capstone imprint

Space Penguins books are published by Stone Arch Books
A Capstone Imprint
1710 Roe Crest Drive
North Mankato, Minnesota 56003
www.capstoneyoungreaders.com

First published by Stripes Publishing Ltd.
1 The Coda Centre
189 Munster Road
London SW6 6AW

Library of Congress Cataloging-in-Publication Data is
available on the Library of Congress website.

ISBN: 978-1-4342-9783-9 (library binding)
ISBN: 978-1-4342-9787-7 (paperback)
ISBN: 978-1-4965-0203-2 (eBook PDF)

Summary: Rocky's reputation for death-defying aerial
acrobatics gains him an invitation to participate in the
galaxy's notorious Superchase Space Race. But will this
turn out to be a race to the death?

Printed in China.
092014   008472RRDS15

TABLE OF CONTENTS

MEET THE SPACE PENGUINS...

CAPTAIN:

James T. Krill
Emperor penguin
Height: 3 ft. 7 in.
Looks: yellow ear patches and noble bearing
Likes: swordfish minus the sword
Lab Test Results: showed leadership qualities in fish challenge
Guaranteed to: keep calm in a crisi

FIRST MATE (ONCE UPON A TIME):

Beaky Wader, now known as Dark Wader
Emperor penguin
Height: 4 ft.
Looks: yellow ear patches and evil laugh
Likes: prawn pizza
Lab Test Results: cheated at every challenge
Guaranteed to: cause trouble

PILOT (WITH NO SENSE OF DIRECTION):

Rocky Waddle

Rockhopper penguin

Height: 1 ft. 6 in.

Looks: long yellow eyebrows

Likes: mackerel ice cream

Lab Test Results: fastest slider in toboggan challenge

Guaranteed to: speed through an asteroid belt while reading charts upside down

SECURITY OFFICER AND HEAD CHEF:

Fuzz Allgrin

Little Blue penguin

Height: 1 ft. 1 in.

Looks: small with fuzzy blue feathers

Likes: fish sticks in cream and truffle sauce

Lab Test Results: showed creativity and aggression in ice-carving challenge

Guaranteed to: defend ship, crew, and kitchen with his life

SHIP'S ENGINEER:

Splash Gordon

King penguin

Height: 3 ft. 1 in.

Looks: orange ears and chest markings

Likes: squid

Lab Test Results: solved ice-cube challenge in under four seconds

Guaranteed to: fix anything

LOADING...

Welcome aboard the spaceship *Tunafish*.
I am ICEcube, the smartest on-board
computer you will ever meet. I guide
my ship and my space crew through the
universe and get them out of *FZZWZZ*.

I mean: trouble.

My circuit boards got wet on our last
mission and are still damp. I keep saying
FZZWZZ for no reason. You have been
warned.

You will be surprised to learn that the
crew on board the *Tunafish* are *FZZWZZ*.

I mean: penguins.

NASA sent me along with five penguins on a top-secret space mission five Earth years ago. We traveled aboard a special fish-shaped spaceship called the *Tunafish*. Then they lost us. My database says: epic failure.

Oh well. Things could be worse. The Space Penguins have kept busy during their time up here. They are now famous across the universe for their intergalactic exploits.

The planet Koffi changed its name to Planet T after Captain James T. Krill's bravery in the famous space battle of Boyling Ketl.

Fuzz Allgrin, Chef and Security Officer, taught the planet Kung-fu-BBQ the difference between a lamb chop and a karate chop.

Splash Gordon, the ship's engineer and inventor, introduced power showers to the stinky aliens on the planet Smelibot.

And the *Tunafish*'s pilot, Rocky Waddle, got lost on the planet Strait-Ahed, which everyone thought was impossible.

Now the Space Penguins just want to find a friendly planet where they can settle down and fish for *FZZWZZ* and slide around on the ice. The trouble is, they keep getting distracted. One minute they're fighting their mortal enemy Dark Wader — an evil penguin robot with plans to rule the universe. The next, they're landing on wet planets, nearly drowning me, and making me say *FZZWZZ* all the time.

Uh-oh. What's this?

An enormous ball of rotting food floating among the stars! And it's right in the *Tunafish*'s path.

I should inform Captain Krill before we crash right into it. But he's busy right now, giving Rocky Waddle some bad news. And Rocky's not looking happy . . .

YUCK!

"The answer is *no*, Rocky," said Captain Krill as the spaceship *Tunafish* cruised through space. They were currently in Section F of the universe, going around three hundred thousand light-years an hour. "You can't enter the Superchase Space Race this year."

"That's what you said last year, Captain!" complained Rocky Waddle. "And the year before. And the year before that!"

"The Superchase Space Race is the most dangerous race in the universe," said

Captain Krill, looking down at his pilot. As an emperor penguin, the captain stood head and flippers above the rest of his crew. "Spaceships get smashed to bits every year. We can't risk losing the *Tunafish* that way. She's the only spaceship we've got."

Splash lifted his inventor's goggles as he joined the conversation. "And the Emperor of Sossij wins every year anyway, doesn't he?" he said. Oil and grime streaked his face, hiding his orange ear patches. "I don't know why anyone else bothers."

"But —" began Rocky.

"Make like a sardine and can it, Rocky," said Fuzz Allgrin. He folded his little blue penguin flippers across his even littler blue penguin tummy. "When Captain Krill says no, he means no."

"Thank you, Fuzz," said Captain Krill.

Rocky slid off his pilot's chair and glared at the other Space Penguins.

He flicked his long yellow eyebrows off his face. "You know what your problem is?" he said. "None of you have any imagination. The winner of the Superchase Space Race wins the Golden Galaxy Goblet — and fame and glory forever! I could win the Superchase Space Race with my eyes closed and my flippers tied behind my back. Everyone knows that I'm the best pilot in outer sp—"

CRASH!

The *Tunafish* shuddered in midair as something smashed into it. Fuzz fell over. Rocky rushed back to his pilot's chair.

"The best pilot in outer space?" said Fuzz, struggling to his feet. "Then how come we just *crashed*?"

"What did we hit, Rocky?" asked Captain Krill.

"I don't know," Rocky admitted, peering through the windshield of the *Tunafish*. "It's gone dark out there."

"We're in *outer space*, trout brains," said Fuzz. "It's always dark out there."

"Darker than normal, I mean," Rocky said. He pointed with one flipper. "What in the name of cod is this stuff?"

Something gloopy was covering the windshield of the *Tunafish*, making it impossible to see out.

"It looks like a thousand moldy squelchglub cores," said Splash.

"By halibut, so it does!" said Fuzz. He stood on his tiptoes to get a better view. "There are lots of old splattergunk peelings as well. And look! Dribblebog guts!"

The squelchglub cores were brown. The splattergunk peelings were nearly black and the dribblebog guts were green. There was lots of other nameless junk smeared across the glass as well. The stench was so strong they could even smell it from inside the spaceship.

"Why have we crashed into a cosmic compost heap, ICEcube?" asked Captain Krill.

"It's not a compost heap, Captain," said ICEcube. "It's space-pig slop."

"Yuck!" cried the Space Penguins.

"The dribblebog guts look great," said Fuzz. "I could turn them into fritters."

"Do you know why there's space-pig slop floating around here, ICEcube?" asked the captain.

"Initiating slop analysis, Captain," said ICEcube.

Captain Krill smoothed his yellow ear patches. "Rocky, move slowly," he said. "And turn on the windshield wipers. Best flippers forward, crew. And . . . go."

ARGOS MEGABUX

Rocky flew the *Tunafish* carefully out of the cloud of space-pig slop. The windshield wipers moved slowly through the muck.

SQUEE . . . squelch. SQUEE . . . squelch.

"Those would make a delicious soup," said Fuzz as several large dribblebog bones slid down the windshield. "I could slip on a spacesuit and collect a few."

"Absolutely not, Fuzz," said Captain Krill firmly.

"I have some information, Captain," said ICEcube. "This pig slop must have come from some kind of weapon. I have detected gunpowder on several of the squelchglub cores. Perhaps the weapon fired a large cannonball of old space food at another spacecraft. The cannonball could have broken up and floated away."

"A cannonball made of old space food?" Captain Krill said. "How extraordinary."

"And there's tons of it!" said Splash. "It must have been *massive*."

"So who fired it?" wondered Fuzz.

"And what were they firing at?" added Splash.

Rocky scanned the horizon in case of another slop-gun attack. Nothing. The *Tunafish* flew onward slowly and carefully. Its windshield wipers were working harder than ever.

SQUEE . . . squelch. SQUEEE . . . squelch. SQUEEEE . . . squelch.

"My heat sensors are detecting a small *FZZWZZ* in the middle of this food field," said ICEcube.

"Spaceship dead ahead!" cried Rocky.

A spaceship of some kind had appeared through the gloom.

It was a sorry sight, dripping with splattergunk peelings and old dribblebog bits. The Space Penguins could barely make out a gleam of white underneath the filth. There was no sign of life through the mucked-up windows.

Captain Krill reached for the communications button. "Mystery spacecraft, this is the *Tunafish*," he said. "Identify yourself."

A weak voice came through the speakers. "Thank the cosmos you're here! This is Argos Megabux of the planet Speedizoom, aboard my race ship, the *Flashaway*. I was heading for the Superchase Space Race when *this* happened. My ship is completely immobilized by filth!"

"How come he gets to go to the Superchase Space Race and I don't?" Rocky grumbled.

"What can we do to help you, Argos Megabux?" Captain Krill asked.

"Get me out of here!" Argos Megabux cried. "I swear, I'm going to be sick. It smells *that* bad. I can't see a thing through the windows. Could you hose me down or something?"

"Splash?" said Captain Krill. "Prime the pressure cannons."

"Right away, Captain," said Splash, waddling off to the engine room. "Tell Megabux to power up the thruster rockets. Our pressure cannons pack a punch."

BLAM BLAM BLAM!

The *Tunafish*'s pressure cannons fired air bullets at Argos Megabux's ship, battering their way through the muck. Slowly but surely, a magnificent spacecraft appeared before the Space Penguins' eyes.

"Wow!" exclaimed Rocky, forgetting to be upset.

The *Flashaway* spun gently in space as the *Tunafish's* pressure cannons pummeled it clean. The ship was a thing of beauty. It had a long neck and a sharp nose. Its neck tapered back to a pure white body, perfectly shaped for speed. The whole thing looked like a dive-bombing swan.

"Great!" came Argos Megabux's voice again. "Now I have to leave before my nostrils explode. Speedizoomians have an excellent sense of smell, so this is torture. We also have a lot of nostrils."

A delicate gray craft was tucked underneath the *Flashaway's* shining body. It looked like a cygnet hitching a ride on its mother's feet. It detached from the *Flashaway* as the Space Penguins watched.

"Thanks, *Tunafish!*" came the voice of Argos Megabux. "I'm out of here!"

The little gray escape craft started jetting away through the food field.

"Hey!" called Fuzz. He stretched his little neck as high as it would go in order to reach the communications button. "You forgot your ship!"

"I never want to smell it again!" came Argos Megabux's voice. "You can have it if you want. As a way of saying thanks."

Rocky almost fell off his pilot's chair. He leaned into the communications speaker. "Seriously? Don't you want it anymore?"

"I'll build another one," said Argos Megabux. "The Superchase Space Race can wait until next year. Right now I just need a shower and a very large rosebush to sniff away this horrible stink. I have the biggest garden on planet Speedizoom, and my plumpi-puff sugar roses are calling me."

The little gray escape craft scorched away in a burst of jet flames, faster than the blink of an eye.

CHAPTER THREE

ENTERING THE RACE

"*Plumpi-puff sugar roses?*" said Fuzz. "What kind of alien was that guy?"

"Did he just give us his race ship?" Rocky asked. "His top-of-the-line race ship? His gorgeous, sleek, fabulous, mega-fast, and extremely expensive race ship? Just because it smells bad?"

"It must be a mistake," said Splash. "He'll be back in a minute to fetch it."

The Space Penguins gazed out through the *Tunafish*'s windshield. Chunks of old squelchglubs bobbed past, but no Argos Megabux. The perfectly white race ship hung among the stars, silent and still.

"Well," said Captain Krill at last. "It looks like it really is ours now."

THUMP.

Rocky slid to the floor.

"I think Rocky just fainted," said Splash. He patted Rocky on the cheeks with his flippers. "*Tunafish* to Rocky Waddle, come in?"

Rocky sat up so suddenly that his beak spiked Splash in the tummy.

"OW!" said Splash.

"This means I can enter the Superchase Space Race!" Rocky said excitedly. "I can race the *Flashaway* instead of the *Tunafish*!"

Captain Krill hesitated. "Well . . ."

"Just *look* at that machine," Rocky said excitedly. "It's designed to win. And with me at the helm, the Golden Galaxy Goblet's in the bag!"

"But it's dangerous!" said Splash.

"Space Penguins love danger!" said Fuzz. "We breathe catastrophe! Our hearts pump to the beat of crashing spaceships! If Rocky blows up with the *Flashaway*, we'll find another pilot. Simple."

"Thanks, Fuzz," said Rocky. He frowned. "I think."

"I'm not saying you *will* explode," Fuzz added. "I actually do think you'll win."

"I still don't like it," said Splash. "What about the slop gun that messed up the *Flashaway* in the first place? We don't know who slopped Megabux, or why. They might come back and slop us instead."

"It was probably just a random space bandit," said Captain Krill. "Argos Megabux was in the wrong place at the wrong time. I don't think we should worry about it, Splash. Let's try this race."

"Scorching scallops!" hooted Rocky. "We're in!"

In the middle of Section E of the universe (which of course is next to Section F), was a bright silver Squid-G fighter. The ship with its long, trailing tentacles scooted through the stars in hot pursuit of the *Tunafish*.

An enormous robot, half penguin and half machine, glided around the Squid-G cabin. His oiled wheels made no sound. He glared through the windshield with laser eyes. It was Dark Wader — renegade penguin and mortal enemy of the Space Penguins!

"Is the signal still coming through, Crabba?" he said to the crab-like creature at the controls of the ship. "Is your jellyfish-cam on the *Tunafish*'s fuselage still sending us the correct coordinates for that tin can of penguins?"

"Yes, boss," said the spiny little alien at the controls. The eyes at the top of its claws blinked at Dark Wader. "There's a new message coming through now."

TUNAFISH HEADING FOR PLANET SOSSIJ IN SECTION G TO ENTER THE SUPERCHASE SPACE RACE.

Dark Wader burst out laughing. "They're entering the Superchase Space Race in that rusty box of scrap metal, the *Tunafish*? They don't stand a chance! Oh, my sides! My sides are splitting!"

There was a crunching noise of breaking metal. Dark Wader stopped laughing.

"Crabba? My sides just split. Weld me back together."

The jellyfish-cam sent a new message.

SPACE PENGUINS ARE ENTERING A RACE SHIP CALLED THE *FLASHAWAY* IN THE SUPERCHASE SPACE RACE. THEY ARE NOT ENTERING THE *TUNAFISH*.

"That changes things," said Dark Wader thoughtfully. The Squid-G hurtled past a large sign that read: WELCOME TO SECTION F OF THE UNIVERSE. FLY SAFELY. "We've never entered the Superchase Space Race, have we, Crabba? Why not?"

"Because the Emperor of Sossij always

wins the Golden Galaxy Goblet," Crabba said. "And you hate losing."

"Maybe this year things will be different," said Dark Wader. "If the Space Penguins think they have a chance in their new race ship, then so do I — in my own sneaky way. Set a course for the planet Sossij at once, Crabba. It's vital that we get there before the *Tunafish*. I have a plan to make this a *sizzling* race!"

CHAPTER FOUR

ANADIN SKYPORKER

Deep in Section G of the universe, the planet Sossij was preparing to host the annual Superchase Space Race.

Flags flew all over the capital city of Bratwurzt. Streamers fluttered from lampposts and trees. Huge billboards beside the roads read: SUPERCHASE SPACE RACE! HEATS TODAY! FINAL TOMORROW! The skies were full of aliens arriving for the big race. It was a colorful sight.

High above Bratwurzt stood the tall towers of the Sossij Imperial Palace. And on the Imperial balcony, near the top of the tallest palace tower, stood the Emperor of Sossij, Anadin Skyporker.

Anadin Skyporker was small and pink. His butterfly-shaped ears twinkled with enormous jewels. His tiny eyes were sharp and his nose was snouty. He wore red shoes with platforms to make himself taller, and a long purple cloak that swirled around his porky shoulders. He looked angry as he gazed down on the bustle of Bratwurzt far below.

"I hate the Superchase Space Race," Skyporker complained. "How many entries this year, Baycon?"

Slyser Baycon was Anadin Skyporker's general. He was taller than the emperor, but he was good at hunching over so that they looked the same height. His cousin, Streeki, was the Superchase Space Race Coordinator. His sister, Smoki, ran the police force. A lot of General Baycon's relatives had important jobs on Sossij.

"Fifty-eight," said General Baycon.

"*What?*" screamed Skyporker.

"We got rid of many of them on their way here," said General Baycon quickly. "We slopped them with our slop guns and they went home."

"Excellent," said Skyporker, calming down. "So how many have made it past the slop guns? One? Two?"

"Twenty-one," said General Baycon. "So far."

Anadin Skyporker had a terrible headache from the heavy jewelry that he wore in his butterfly ears. It made him extra temperamental.

"*Twenty-one?*" he screamed. "Tell them all to go away, Baycon! The Golden Galaxy Goblet is *mine*!"

SUPERCHASE
SPACE RACE

HEATS TODAY!
FINAL TOMORROW!

The emperor threw himself to the ground and pounded the floor with his polished hooves in a furious rage.

"You will win the same as always, Your Imperial Pigness," General Baycon promised. "Your only real competition this year was the *Flashaway* — the race ship belonging to Argos Megabux from the planet Speedizoom. We slopped that one in Section F of the universe yesterday. We won't be seeing Megabux this year. And our Breakfast Banquet will deal with anyone else who squeezes past the slop guns."

Anadin Skyporker forgot about his headache. "Good news!" he said, getting up again. "And you're sure that poisoning everyone at this Breakfast Banquet will work? Isn't it easier just to make them crash as normal?"

"People are getting suspicious about all the crashes," said General Baycon. "We needed a new approach."

Skyporker trotted over to the large glass case that stood in the middle of the Imperial balcony. The Golden Galaxy Goblet gleamed through the glass. It was shiny and huge and very, very golden.

"Then I'll win you all over again, dear Golden Galaxy Goblet," said Skyporker happily. He threw open his little piggy arms. "I love the Superchase Space Race."

A bright ship suddenly appeared over the Imperial balcony, its silver tentacles trailing behind it. It landed on the Imperial space-pad at the top of the tallest palace tower.

"Dark Wader, of the space station *Death Starfish*," announced a Sossij guard at the doors of the Imperial balcony.

Dark Wader glided in with Crabba on his metal shoulder. "Greetings, Your Imperial Sossij-ness," said Wader. "I am Dark Wader, and this is my assistant, Crabba."

Anadin Skyporker's headache was back. He glared at the huge black pengbot and crabby alien in front of him. "What do you want?"

"I want to help you win the Superchase Space Race," said Dark Wader. "Because only I can show you how to beat the Space Penguins."

Anadin Skyporker gave a start. "The Space Penguins? Those intergalactic hero birds are entering the Superchase Space Race? I hate heroes. They make my snout twitch. Do you know anything about this, General Baycon?"

"I believe the Space Penguins fly a rustbucket of a ship called the *Tunafish*," said General Baycon. "It's no match for your own magnificent race craft, the *Krakling*."

"You're right. The penguins' normal spaceship is useless," said Crabba from Dark Wader's shoulder. "But they aren't racing the *Tunafish*. They're racing a ship by the name of *Flashaway*."

"Impossible!" General Baycon sputtered. "I slopped — er, I know for a fact that the *Flashaway* isn't entering the race."

They all heard the rumbling sound of engines overhead. A rusty, fish-shaped spacecraft came into view, towing a beautiful swan-like race ship. The word *Flashaway* gleamed over the Imperial balcony for a moment, before the *Tunafish* banked gently and headed toward the starting line. The smell of rotten food followed the *Flashaway* in a stinky cloud.

"Impossible," General Baycon repeated faintly.

Anadin Skyporker could feel the mother of all headaches coming on. "Go away, Wader," he said. "I will win the race as usual — without your help. I have a fail-safe plan. Those penguins don't stand a chance!"

Dark Wader's eyes glinted. "Have it your way, Your Imperialness. We'll talk again when it all goes wrong."

CHAPTER FIVE

A POISONOUS INVITATION

The *Tunafish* approached the Superchase
Space Race starting line.

"I'm sure I saw a Squid-G fighter on top
of that tall tower back there," said Splash.

"Only Dark Wader flies Squid-Gs, Splash,"
said Fuzz. "And we're a million light years
away from Wader's space station."

"You must be seeing things," said
Captain Krill.

Rocky steered the *Tunafish* and the

Flashaway into a perfect landing beside a river flowing toward the city center. They passed other race ships as they taxied along. There were big shiny golden ones, tiny black disc-shaped ones, red ones and purple ones and blue ones, all with names like *Whizzer* and *Lightning* and *Gosh I'm Fast.*

As soon as the *Tunafish* and the *Flashaway* stopped, admiring race-goers surrounded the pure white race ship.

"Wow!"

"It's a Speedizoom Megabux Model Twelve! Smells kinda funny, though."

"I didn't think anyone in the universe could afford one of these!"

Rocky tossed his eyebrows. "Leave this to me, guys," he said. "The Rockmeister has everything under control."

"The *Rockmeister*?" said Fuzz. Rocky hopped off the *Tunafish* and straight into the cheering crowds. "That rockhopper's getting too big for his flippers. He wants us to leave all the fun and admiration to him? No way, stingray!"

Splash, Captain Krill, and Fuzz jumped out of the *Tunafish* and stood blinking in the bright Sossij sunlight. Alien rock music blasted their ears. Multi-colored aliens of different shapes and sizes had already gathered around Rocky, clapping him on the back with arms, legs, and other limbs.

"You have some fine stinky wings there, my friend!"

"Is it faster than the Megabux Model Eleven?"

"This baby is faster than a rocket with a rocket strapped to its back," Rocky boasted.

"Ooh!" said the crowd. They loved a bit of boasting.

"Your name and the name of your race ship, please," said a race marshal.

"Rocky Waddle and the *Flashaway*, here

to enter the Superchase Space Race," said Rocky. He smirked. "Sorry — here to *win* the Superchase Space Race."

"Ooh!" said the crowd again.

Captain Krill tried to get Rocky's attention, but the rockhopper was enjoying himself too much.

"He's signing autographs and the race hasn't even started!" said Splash.

"Maybe letting Rocky enter this race was a bad idea," said Fuzz. "We're a team, not a one-penguin band."

The loudspeakers over the Space Penguins' heads stopped pumping out alien rock. A voice crackled out instead.

"This is your race coordinator, Streeki Baycon, speaking. The Racers' Breakfast Banquet will take place in the Banquet Hall of the Imperial Palace at precisely nine o'clock this morning. All race pilots are ordered — I mean, invited to attend. Long live His Generous Pigness, Emperor Anadin Skyporker!"

"Skyporker!" shouted the crowd. "Long live the emperor!"

The crowd surged away from the race runway toward the Imperial Palace, taking Rocky with them.

"Rocky!" called Captain Krill. "Wait for us!"

But Rocky was lost in the crowd.

"At times like this, I wish we could fly," grumbled Splash. "We need to stay close and keep an eye on him."

Captain Krill pointed to the river. "We'll swim to the Imperial Palace and meet Rocky there."

The Space Penguins squeezed through the pressing crowd to the edge of the water. Then they jumped in.

"This is the way to travel!" said Fuzz. He swooped in and out of the river with his flippers pressed to his sides and his feet whizzing like bicycle pedals through the gently flowing current. "Who needs roads?"

Captain Krill was the first to jump out of the river as it flowed beside the golden gates of the Imperial Palace. He brushed the water off his white tummy. The other penguins jumped out and joined him on the riverbank.

"The clock over the palace gates says it's twenty to nine," the captain told the others. "We're early."

The penguins gawked at the great courtyard of the Imperial Palace. It was *huge.* It was also empty, apart from a few piggy-looking Sossij waiters carrying large dishes of food inside.

"So, where's this Banquet Hall?" said Fuzz.

"Follow the waiters," Splash suggested.

"You're a genius, Splash," said Captain Krill.

Splash shrugged his shoulders. "I know."

The penguins hopped up the steps and through the mighty front door.

"Stop," Captain Krill said suddenly, pulling the others to one side.

In the hall, a large Sossij guard was sprinkling green powder on each platter of food as the waiters marched inside.

"Funny-looking salt," said Fuzz.

"Salt isn't green," said Splash. "That must be poison! I invented something similar to use on my fleas yesterday."

"Did it work?" said Fuzz.

"It killed them all stone dead!" said Splash.

"So why are they poisoning the food for the Breakfast Banquet?" asked Fuzz.

"I don't like the look of this," said Captain Krill. "Keep following the waiters, crew. And stay out of sight."

CHAPTER SIX

GOING BOWLING

The palace hallways were lined with pictures of the Sossij emperor in heavy gold frames. They all showed him dressed in his Imperial finery, standing on victory podiums, and waving the Golden Galaxy Goblet.

Captain Krill paused for a moment, looking at them thoughtfully.

The penguins came to the bottom of a very long spiral staircase. The Sossij waiters were almost out of sight, near the top.

"Start hopping, crew," said Captain Krill.

The Imperial staircase went on forever. The penguins reached the top, panting and out of breath. Another staircase, just as long and twisty as the first one, lay ahead of them.

"Oh *great*," said Fuzz. "More stairs."

Suddenly, something came skidding around the bend and came face to face with the captain.

"Crabba!" Captain Krill yelled.

"Penguin!" Crabba yelled back.

"What are you doing here, crusty-face?" Fuzz demanded.

"I *knew* I saw a Squid-G!" said Splash. "Wader must be here!"

The eyes on the ends of Crabba's claws glinted. "It's been very nice chatting, but now I'm going to nick you with my deadly pinchers."

SNAP!

"Don't let him bite you," said Splash, dancing out of the way.

"No kidding, haddock chops," said Fuzz.

SNAP! SNAP! The snappy alien came closer.

"Dark Wader will be very pleased if I can get rid of you all," he said with a grin. "He plans to win the Superchase Space Race, you see. And you're in the way. But one little pinch from my pinchers and it's bye-bye Space Penguins."

SNAP! SNAP! SNAP!

"We'll never get out of this alive," Splash cried.

"Never say never," said the captain. "Follow me!"

SNAP!

Crabba's poisonous claws met thin air as Captain Krill leaped upward, twisting around mid-jump. His white belly hit the smooth silver banister of the Imperial staircase and he started to slide.

"Crazy codfish," whooped Fuzz, jumping after the captain. "This looks even more fun than fighting!"

"No!" Crabba roared as Splash leaped onto the banister, too.

But there was no way the crabby villain could catch the Space Penguins now. The banister curved and curled, twisting around and around. The penguins sped along, the air whistling over their backs as they went

faster . . . faster . . . faster . . . heading for
the bottom.

"Watch out for the knobby thing!"
shouted Splash. "I saw it on our way up!"

"What knobby thing?" Fuzz shouted
back.

"*That* knobby thing!" cried Captain Krill.

A silver ball topped the end of the
banister. The Space Penguins were going to
smash right into it!

Captain Krill sprang into the air and
somersaulted over the silver ball at the very
last moment. Fuzz just scraped over the top.
Splash jumped so high that he almost hit
the spiky chandelier near the ceiling. All
three penguins landed on the thick Imperial
carpet with muffled thumps.

They had landed next to a gleaming
elevator with a row of silver buttons. Next
to this was a sign that read: No Waiters
Allowed.

Captain Krill reached for the button right at the top, marked Banquet Hall. "Get in," he ordered. "And watch out for Crabba."

"How come we didn't see this elevator first time around?" Fuzz complained.

The elevator rocketed the penguins upward. *PING.*

They stepped out into the Banquet Hall.

They stared at the hollowed-out tables lining the grand room.

"Those tables look like pig troughs," said Splash.

"The Emperor of Sossij looks like a pig," Captain Krill said. "He probably eats like one, too."

"Do you think the waiters will just dump all the banquet food in the troughs together?" asked Fuzz, wrinkling his beak. "The main course and dessert and everything?"

"The waiters aren't going to get that far," said Captain Krill. "No one's going to be poisoned today."

"But how can we stop them?" said Splash.

Captain Krill smiled. "Let's go bowling."

The first waiters appeared. They were panting with the effort of carrying their shiny platters of food up two massive flights of stairs to the Banquet Hall. The penguins noticed that the greenish color of the poisonous sprinkles had faded away.

The waiters' eyes widened as they saw the penguins waiting for them on the top step.

"Hello," said Captain Krill. "And goodbye!"

He pushed the first waiter backward.

BUMP-BUMP-BUMP-CRASH went the waiter, falling back down the stairs and knocking over a few more waiters on the way.

"See?" said Captain Krill. "Bowling."

"This is my kind of game," said Fuzz. "Ninja penguin!"

Fuzz's flying feet caught two more waiters on their piggy chins. They knocked over twelve more waiters still coming up the stairs. And those twelve knocked over twelve more.

BANG! CRASH! CRUNCH!

The Space Penguins karate chopped waiters left and right, sending them flying back down the stairs. Food went everywhere.

BANG! CRASH! CRUNCH! CRASH! BANGGG!

The noise of waiters and plates bouncing down the stairs was tremendous. Finally, the penguins heard the sound of one last big silver plate clonking into someone at the bottom. Then there was silence.

"I think that was the last of them," said Splash.

PING. The elevator door opened. A waiter stepped out, carrying his platter nervously over his head.

"Using the elevator?" Fuzz said. "Naughty, naughty." He chopped the startled waiter at the knees and knocked him to the ground. "*That* was the last of them."

"The emperor's going to be madder than an electric eel when he sees this mess," said Splash.

"Good," said Captain Krill. "I don't like cheaters."

"Who cheated?" said Fuzz. He looked at

the groaning waiter by his feet. "Okay, this waiter cheated by taking the elevator. But that's a stupid rule, anyway."

"Remember all those pictures of the emperor posing with the Golden Galaxy Goblet?" said the captain. "It made me wonder . . . how does he win the goblet every single year?"

"By flying really well?" said Fuzz.

"By cheating!" Splash exclaimed.

"The emperor poisoned this food to make sure he'd win the race today," Captain Krill said. "Thanks to the Space Penguins, this is going to be the first fair Superchase Space Race in a very long time."

CHAPTER SEVEN

DARK WADER'S EVIL PLAN

The Space Penguins whizzed back down the Imperial banisters. By the time they reached the bottom, the Breakfast Banquet-goers were starting to arrive at the palace.

"Rocky!" Fuzz shouted, almost cannoning into his rockhopper space-mate. "There you are! You totally *have* to try these banisters."

"Where did you guys go?" Rocky complained. "A pilot needs his team! I've been waiting for *ages*."

"We've been a little busy," said Captain Krill. "As you can see."

"*You* made this mess?" Rocky said, looking at the plates, food, and groaning waiters scattered on the floor. "Why?"

"The emperor poisoned the banquet," Splash said. "So we wrecked it."

"That's the biggest load of garbage I've ever heard," Rocky said angrily. "Why would the emperor do that?"

"Because he's a *cheater*, squid skull," said Fuzz.

"You're just jealous," Rocky said. "You're jealous because I've been getting all the attention around here."

"Take that back!" shouted Fuzz.

"No!" Rocky yelled. "I was really looking forward to that banquet and now you've *ruined* it!"

Things were also going badly on the Imperial balcony.

"What?" Anadin Skyporker's piggy face was bright red with fury. "*All* of it? *All* the poisoned banquet food? Gone?"

"I'm afraid so, Your Imperial Pigness," said General Baycon. "There seems to have been a massive accident on the Imperial staircase."

"No!" screamed Skyporker. He felt like he had an angry space sprongle inside his head. "No one ate the food! That means . . . That means . . ."

"You'll have to race twenty-two other pilots to win the Golden Galaxy Goblet, Your Imperial Pigness," said General Baycon. "Including the Space Penguins' late entry."

"NOOO!" Anadin Skyporker had the loudest tantrum the planet of Sossij had ever heard. The Golden Galaxy Goblet shook in its glass case. The guards at the doors of the Imperial balcony covered their ears.

"We should have made them all crash like we usually do!" Anadin Skyporker screeched. "Now there's no time to tamper with the race ships and make them crash! I'm very, very *annoyed*!"

"Don't worry, Your Ham-Sandwichness," said Dark Wader, gliding onto the Imperial balcony. "Everything is under control. I sent

Crabba to plant space mines around the racecourse. I'll give you a map of where they are. The Space Penguins are the ones who wrecked your banquet, by the way. I told you they were tricky."

"You've planted space mines! You're a marvel, Wader!" Sykporker said in delight. As if by magic, Skyporker's tantrum had stopped. "How can I reward you? I'll give you anything! What about General Baycon's job?"

"What?" said General Baycon.

Dark Wader brushed a little dust off his blinking electronic chest. "I want to enter the race," he said smoothly.

"But then I'll have to race against twenty-*three* pilots!" wailed Skyporker.

"They'll all blow up in the heats," said Wader. "We'll be the only two ships in the final, Skyporker. You and me. One on one. What do you say?"

Wader's just a big metal penguin, Anadin Skyporker thought cunningly. *I could probably chuck a glass of water at his chest and he'd go bang . . .*

"It's a deal, Wader," Skyporker said with a snouty smile.

Down at the racecourse, it was time for the heats to begin.

Anadin Skyporker stroked the nose of his Imperial red race ship, the *Krakling*.

He glared at the twenty-three other race ships lined up along the Superchase Space Race starting line. He glared especially hard at the *Flashaway*, gleaming brightly nearby.

Anadin buckled himself into his golden race suit and climbed into the *Krakling's* jeweled cabin. As he settled himself down at the controls, he pressed his communications button. "You'd better be right about blowing up everyone else, Wader," he pouted. "And it being just you and me in the final."

"Trust me, Skyporker," said Dark Wader. He flashed an evil smile from the shiny silver cabin of the Squid-G parked beside the *Krakling*. "We'll destroy everyone. And there will be penguin-shaped fireworks today."

The loudspeaker crackled to life. "We have six heats, with four race ships competing in each heat," said Streeki Baycon. "Anyone who completes their heat will move on to the Superchase Space Race final tomorrow morning. If everyone explodes — I mean, crashes — there won't be a Superchase Space Race final and the Emperor Anadin Skyporker will keep the Golden Galaxy Goblet for another year. Long live His Imperial Pigness! Heat One, start your engines!"

CHAPTER EIGHT

BANG!

The Superchase Space Race course went straight up through the atmosphere of Sossij. When it reached outer space, it rocketed around the moon of Rynd and through the asteroid field of Salami, past the Black Hole of Pudyng, then whipped back through the meteor shower of Meatior. The whole loop ended back at the starting line in Bratwurzt. It was a tricky course to pilot even without the space mines that Dark Wader had planted along the way.

The sixteen race ships in Heats One to Four had already zoomed away. No one had made it back to the finish line yet. Plumes of smoke drifted ominously through the sky.

Anadin Skyporker hummed aboard the *Krakling*, winking at Dark Wader in the Squid-G fighter next to him. Rocky was scheduled for Heat Five. The emperor and Dark Wader were in Heat Six.

The Space Penguins had glimpsed Dark Wader at the starting line a little earlier. The pengbot had ignored them, which was strange.

"Heat Five, start your engines," Streeki Baycon said through the loudspeaker.

Rocky waved at the cheering spectators and climbed aboard the *Flashaway*.

"For the last time, Rocky, you have to *listen* to us," Captain Krill called up to him. "No one has finished a heat yet. Doesn't that make you suspicious?"

"They're all bad pilots," said Rocky. "I knew that already."

"The emperor is up to something!" Splash insisted. "Those plumes of smoke coming out of the sky smell like dynamite."

"La-la-la, I'm not listening," Rocky said, buckling himself into the *Flashaway*.

"You idiotic iceberg!" shouted Fuzz. "You pickled herring! You *fish stick*!

We're trying to help you!"

"Tell it to the flipper, cuz the beak ain't listening," said Rocky, closing the door.

BANG!

The starting pistol cracked through the air. The *Flashaway* zoomed down the runway, followed by three other ships: the *Zoom Baby*, the *Buzzer*, and the *Whizzer*.

Within a few seconds, they had rocketed up, up, up . . . and out of sight.

Rocky loved being at the controls of the *Flashaway*. Every button he pressed did something exciting. The racing engines purred away underneath him as he raced upward. He was ahead of the other ships already and the race had just started.

The sky changed from blue to black as

Rocky hit the stratosphere. Lights blinked brightly on the *Flashaway*'s dashboard.

"I'm in space, winning a race, it's totally ace," sang Rocky, whizzing around the moon of Rynd.

The planet Sossij looked tiny by now. Rocky studied the star map on the dashboard. Where was he? The asteroid field of Salami was supposed to be right here, but it wasn't. There weren't any spectators up here watching the race ships, either. He thought there'd be *tons*.

What was the point of winning a race if no one was watching?

Rocky saw some asteroids looming on the great black horizon. They looked a little like the asteroid field on his map. Maybe not exactly, but . . .

"Close enough," Rocky decided.

He gunned the *Flashaway*'s engines and headed that direction. It was bound to be right. How many asteroid fields could hang around one planet, for kipper's sake?

"Tra-la-la," sang Anadin Skyporker, sitting at the starting line behind the controls of the *Krakling*.

"Everything's going according to plan, Crabba," Dark Wader told his small, crabby pilot aboard the Squid-G. "Soon the Space Penguins will be no more."

"You do realize Rocky Waddle's the only penguin aboard the *Flashaway*, don't you, boss?" said Crabba.

Dark Wader waved a metal flipper at his little sidekick. "Of course I do. But when Rocky goes bang, the others won't have a pilot anymore. They'll be history. They'll have to stay on Sossij forever. No more

space hero stuff for them. HAHAHAHA —
Oh, poo! My sides just split again."

The Space Penguins waited tensely by the
finish line for Rocky to return. Not one single
race ship had made it back yet.

BANG. The Space Penguins heard the distant
sound of an explosion high above them. Two
more quickly followed. *BANG. BANG.*

"Nineteen explosions so far," said Captain
Krill grimly. "Rocky could be number
twenty."

There was a gasp from the
crowd as a race ship suddenly
shot out of the clouds toward
them. It was moving
so quickly that it
was difficult

to tell at first what color it was. Then the penguins saw it. It was white. It was fast.

It was the *Flashaway*!

The crowd was roaring as the *Flashaway* approached the finish line.

"Anchovies away!" yelled Splash as Captain Krill waved his flippers in the air in an un-captain-like way. "Rocky's moved on to the Superchase Space Race final!"

"Rocky the Rockmeister *rocks*!" screamed Fuzz.

A different sort of screaming was going on aboard the *Krakling*, where Dark Wader and Crabba had joined the emperor and General Baycon to watch the conclusion of Heat Five.

"How did he do it?" howled Anadin Skyporker. "How did he get past the space mines in the asteroid field of Salami? How did he avoid the pull of the Black Hole of Pudyng and the fiery meteors of Meatior? You're fired, General Baycon! You're *fired*, Wader! Everyone on this planet is totally fired!"

"There's a well-known expression among penguins, Your Imperial Pigness," said Dark Wader as the *Flashaway* approached. He smiled, his metal beak flashing in the sunlight that poured through the windshield of the *Krakling*. "Don't count your icebergs until they've melted."

BANG!

As its nose crossed the finish line, the *Flashaway* exploded.

CHAPTER NINE

ROCKY SAYS SORRY

The *Flashaway* broke in two. The front end somersaulted once, twice, then landed upside down.

"OOH!" gasped the crowd.

"I planted the last space mine on the finish line," Dark Wader said. "Just in case."

"You really are seriously evil, boss," said Crabba, clicking his claws together.

"I'm sorry I ever doubted you, Wader!" beamed Anadin Skyporker. "Are you sure you don't want General Baycon's job?"

"I just want you to fly a fair race in our heat, Skyporker," said Wader. He raised his metal eyebrows and looked down at the emperor. "You are going to fly fair, aren't you?"

"Of course I'm going to fly fair!" Skyporker spluttered. "I'm going to fly fair and *win*!"

Dark Wader left the *Krakling* and clanked aboard his Squid-G. "Watch Skyporker, Crabba," he ordered. "I don't trust him."

As he shut the ship's door, a large glass of water, which had been balancing on top of the door, tipped over and landed on Dark Wader's head.

"Oh, and Crabba? Fetch me a towel."

"There's been a change to the line-up of Heat Six," said Streeki Baycon through the loudspeaker. "The *Breakneck* and the *Speedolite* have decided they don't want to race anymore and are going home to their mommies. What's left of Heat Six, start your engines. Long live the emperor!"

As the *Krakling* and the Squid-G fighter zoomed away, Captain Krill waddled over to the smoking wreckage of the *Flashaway*. Splash and Fuzz followed after him, imagining the worst.

Rocky's seatbelt was holding him upside down in the pilot's chair, his eyebrows dangling. Amazingly, he had hardly dented a feather.

"Did I do it?" asked

Rocky weakly as they dragged him out. "Did I make the final?"

"Great beluga buttocks, of course you did!" said Fuzz. "You're the Rockmeister!"

"The damage doesn't look too bad," Splash said. "I should be able to put those two halves back together in time for the final, as long as it doesn't —"

KABOOOOM!

Both parts of the *Flashaway* went up in two spectacular balls of flame.

"— completely explode," finished Splash.

"It just completely exploded!" Rocky said in dismay.

Race officials scurried onto the runway with dustpans and brushes to sweep up the remains of the mighty Megabux Model Twelve.

Rocky's eyebrows drooped. "How am I going to win the final without the *Flashaway*?"

"You're not," said Fuzz. "Hard herrings, Rocky."

"I'm sorry, guys," Rocky said miserably. "I should have listened when you told me the emperor was a cheat. He and Dark Wader must have planted space mines all over the course. I'm as selfish as a shellfish and I don't deserve a team like you."

"Apology accepted, Rocky," said Captain Krill.

"How come you didn't blow up earlier like everyone else?" Splash asked.

"I went the wrong way. I only found the course again right at the end."

"That explains a lot," said Fuzz.

"This isn't over yet, Rocky," Captain Krill said.

"But I can't race in the final without a ship!"

Captain Krill looked at the rusty *Tunafish*, standing in the space-parking lot beside the race runway. "We can't let Skyporker and Wader get away with this," he said. "You'll have to use the *Tunafish* instead."

The others gasped.

"But what if I mess things up?" asked Rocky. "We won't have a spaceship!"

"It's a risk worth taking," said Captain Krill. "The honor of the Space Penguins is at stake!"

The Squid-G raced over the finish line moments before the *Krakling*.

"And the winner of Heat Six is . . . the squid-like ship with tentacles!" shouted Streeki Baycon through the loudspeaker.

The crowd went nuts.

"I *hate* losing!" shouted Anadin Skyporker, unbuckling himself from the *Krakling* in a rage. His head thumped like a

rock concert. "What happened to that glass of water I balanced on the door of Wader's spaceship?"

"It seems that Dark Wader is waterproof, Your Imperialness," said General Baycon. He bent his knees a little more than normal. "This race was only the qualifying heat, though. The main thing is that you're through to the final."

"Make sure my slop guns on the moon of Rynd are primed and pointing at Wader," Skyporker hissed. "That metal penguin is getting up my snout. Nothing will give me more pleasure than blasting him out of the sky with a ball of old dribblebog guts."

"This is officially the most exciting Superchase Space Race ever!" said Streeki Baycon through the loudspeaker as the crowd cheered wildly. "Three race ships are through to the final, folks! That's more race ships than ever before!"

"*Three?*" yelled the emperor.

"The third ship belongs to the penguins, sir," said General Baycon.

Skyporker boggled at his general. "But their ship blew up! I saw it!"

"Apparently they're going to race the *Tunafish* instead," said Baycon.

Skyporker relaxed. "I saw that pathetic ship in the space-parking lot before the race," he giggled, rubbing his hooves together. "Nothing to worry us, eh, Baycon?"

"Nothing at all, sir," he agreed.

CHAPTER TEN

GET SET, GO!

It was a long night for the Space Penguins as Splash worked on the *Tunafish*, turning her from an old rustbucket to a slightly less rusty old race ship. He was busy hammering and screwing and soldering extra bits of the *Tunafish* together in the bright Sossij moonlight. Rocky kept to himself, polishing the nose of the *Tunafish* until it gleamed.

"Rocky's very quiet," Captain Krill said to Splash.

Splash pulled up his goggles. "He's learned an important lesson, Captain," he said. "The Space Penguins work best as a team."

"Do you think we can win this race in the *Tunafish*?" Captain Krill asked.

"I'd like to say yes," said Splash. "But it's unlikely."

"ICEcube?" said the captain.

"My database says: fat *FZZWZZ*," said ICEcube.

"Fish soup!" Fuzz announced. He waddled out of the *Tunafish*, carrying four soup bowls along his flippers. "It's my special recipe."

After their dinner, the penguins went back to work. There was still a lot to do, and sunrise was only a few hours away.

The morning of the final dawned. The
crowds were larger and louder than ever.
Pennants fluttered. Sossij traders walked
around, selling slop snacks and mud
massages as the *Tunafish*, the *Krakling*, and
the Squid-G fighter lined up at the starting
line.

"Welcome to the Superchase Space Race
Final!" said Streeki Baycon through the
loudspeaker.

"Here goes, team," said Rocky. "I can't do this without you. One for all . . ."

"And all for *FISH*!" cheered the others.

"On your marks," said Streeki Baycon.

"Slop Wader at the first opportunity, General Baycon!" Skyporker hissed into his communications button as he revved the *Krakling*'s engines.

"Get set," said Streeki Baycon.

"I've sent out two mechanical mega-meteors to the meteor shower of Meatior, Crabba," said Dark Wader as Crabba flipped a couple of switches. "And there's a space mine by the finish line again, just in case. If we don't win this race, I shall be extremely surprised."

"Go!" shouted Streeki Baycon.

VROOOOOM!

The Squid-G leaped into the air. The *Krakling* gave chase. Rocky pressed hard on the thruster and the *Tunafish* took off.

The penguins leaned back in their seats as it rocketed through the stratosphere, the mesosphere, and finally into the black emptiness of space itself.

Strings of spaceships lined the route, with flags attached for the competitors to see. Aliens cheered from inside their cabins. If sound could travel in space, it would have been extremely noisy.

"Head for the asteroid field of Salami, Rocky," Captain Krill ordered as they

GO PENGUINS!

whizzed around the moon of Rynd. "We want the second field, not the first."

"That's where I went wrong!" exclaimed Rocky. "Well, there and a couple of other places."

"Snacks, anyone?" said Fuzz from the kitchen.

The asteroid field of Salami was scary. Some of the asteroids were tiny, while others were the size of mountains. All of them were moving extremely fast.

"Dodging space rocks is so refreshing," said Dark Wader, leading the race. "Don't you agree, Crabba?"

Crabba heaved the joystick of the spaceship, narrowly missing a pointy-looking asteroid. "Whatever you say, boss," he panted.

Anadin Skyporker had never had to race this fast in his life. The rusty little *Tunafish* was about to overtake the *Krakling*, the Squid-G fighter was almost out of sight and the asteroid field of Salami was whizzing toward him like a crazy stone fireworks display.

"Shoot them, Baycon!" he screamed into his communications speaker. "Shoot them *both*

"Right away, Your Imperialness!" General Baycon said.

BANG-SPLAT!

A slop gun splattered the tentacles of the Squid-G. Dark Wader felt the ship rock from side to side. The stinky remains of the cannonball squelched onto the vast cliffface of a nearby asteroid.

"That nasty little cheater is shooting at us from the moon of Rynd," Wader said, looking out of the window. "What a surprise."

The *Tunafish* was catching up. But then — *BANG-SPLAT!*

CHAPTER ELEVEN

WHOOPS!

"Whiffing winkles!" yelled Fuzz as the *Tunafish*'s windows went black. "I recognize that stench. The slop gun that got the *Flashaway* — it was Skyporker! And now he's turning it on us. What a stinky thing to do."

"Windshield wipers on full, Rocky," said Splash. "I added a booster button last night!"

SQUEE . . . squelch! SQUEE . . . squelch! SQUEE . . . squelch! SQUEE . . . squelch!

BANG-SPLAT! BANG-SPLAT!

"You can't catch me, Skyporker!" shouted Rocky. He pulled on the joystick. The *Tunafish* jumped like a dolphin, just missing two stinking balls of slop as they hurtled past.

"AAARGH!" screamed Skyporker, trailing behind. "Wader and the penguins got past the slop guns! Do something, General Baycon!"

"The Black Hole of Pudyng will finish them off, Your Royal Pigness," said General Baycon in a reassuring voice.

Unlike the action-packed asteroid field of Salami, the Black Hole of Pudyng sat like an enormous spider at the center of a great empty web of space. Speed was good, but so was caution. If the race ships passed too close to the black hole's great unblinking eye, they would be sucked up and crunched into nothing.

"Here we go!" roared Rocky, slamming on the thruster. "We have to go close, guys, so hold your breath!"

The Space Penguins felt the chill of the Black Hole of Pudyng as they belted past. Rocky had steered them clear of the black hole's terrible pull — but only just.

"NOOOO!" squealed Skyporker. He had kept a good distance away from the black hole, hoping the giant space whirlpool would grind his enemies into dust. Now he was farther behind than ever.

"We've only got the meteor shower of Meatior to go, crew!" cried Captain Krill.

The sky burst into flames as the meteors of Meatior zoomed past the *Tunafish* like fiery arrows.

"Watch out, Rocky!" said Splash, clinging to his goggles for dear life. "There's a meteor. There's another. And there's another!"

The *Tunafish* galloped through the flaming meteors of Meatior like a seahorse. Dark Wader's Squid-G fighter was still ahead, but Rocky was closing the gap. Then —

KABOOOM!

A strange-looking meteor with a flaming

red tail exploded right beside the *Tunafish*, which flipped over like an omelet. Rocky kept his flippers on the joystick until the spaceship was the right way up again.

"That wasn't a meteor," said Captain Krill. "Skyporker's cheating again. Keep your eyes peeled for any more meteors with red tails, crew!"

"Aye, aye, Captain!"

Skyporker dipped after the *Tunafish*. His head was like a hive of angry hornets and he was sweating like — well, like a pig.

"I don't *care* if we don't have any slop left, Baycon!" he screeched into his communications button. "Make some! I — am — losing — this — race!"

As the *Tunafish* dived between the last burning meteors and back toward the Bratwurzt runway, another meteor with a tail of bright red flames gave chase.

"Flippers on full, Rocky!" Captain Krill shouted. "Don't let that red-tailed meteor get us!"

The *Tunafish* spun like an ice-skater, missing the red flaming mega-meteor by the whisker of a catfish. They were flying so fast they had almost caught up with the Squid-G.

"AARGH!" the emperor screamed as he entered the atmosphere of Sossij.

KABOOOOM!

The *Krakling* hit the mega-meteor, which exploded. Pieces of red race craft flew into the air. For the first time in his life, Emperor Anadin Skyporker, the space pig, discovered what it felt like to fly.

"Watch out, Crabba!" roared Dark Wader, his laser eyes widening with shock.

WALLOP!

The broken nose of the *Krakling* struck the Squid-G right in its silver belly.

"Whoops," said Crabba and sat on his claws to hide his eyes.

The Squid-G fighter zoomed downward and hit the ground hard.

CRRRRUNCH!

"Oh, poo!" screamed Dark Wader.

His race for the Golden Galaxy Goblet was over.

CHAPTER TWELVE

VICTORY!

The windows of Bratwurzt shook in their frames. Race ships tooted their horns. Fireworks exploded in the Sossij sky.

"PEN-GUINS! PEN-GUINS! PEN-GUINS!" roared the crowd as the Space Penguins stood on the winners' podium, waving proudly.

"I'm pleased to present Rocky Waddle with the Golden Galaxy Goblet," announced Streeki Baycon. "Winner of this year's Superchase Space Race!"

"PEN-GUINS! PEN-GUINS! PEN-GUINS!"

Rocky stepped forward to receive the great golden cup. "Thanks," he said. "But I want to give the Goblet to my captain, Captain James T. Krill. He made this whole thing possible."

"PEN-GUINS! PEN-GUINS!"

Captain Krill took the Goblet. "Thank you, Rocky," he said. "But I think it should go to Splash Gordon for his hard work on the *Tunafish* last night."

"PEN-GUINS! PEN-GUINS!"

"And *I* think it should go to Fuzz Allgrin for his excellent fish soup," said Splash, handing the Golden Galaxy Goblet over yet again.

"I'll accept it for everyone," said Fuzz. "The Space Penguins are a team, after all. And I shall mix a fish cocktail in the Golden Galaxy Goblet tonight to celebrate!"

P.S.

Dark Wader and Anadin Skyporker limped toward the finish line. It was getting dark.

"I hate the Superchase Space Race," said Skyporker bitterly. "I hate you, too, Wader. But most of all . . . I hate those Space Penguins."

"I bet you don't hate them as much as I do, you pathetic porky pipsqueak," growled Wader.

"I'm a pathetic porky *emperor*, not a pathetic porky pipsqueak!" screeched Skyporker. He was having the worst day of his life.

"My armor is cracked and my ship has exploded and my butt hurts and if I want to call you a pipsqueak I will call you a pipsqueak!" shouted Wader. "Now, I'm going to sit down at the finish line and take a little break. I deserve it."

"Don't sit there, boss," said Crabba
suddenly from his usual perch on his boss's
shoulder. "That's where we put the last
space m—"

KABOOOOM!

"Oh, poo . . ."

ABOUT THE AUTHOR

LUCY COURTENAY has been writing children's fiction for a long time. She's written for book series like The Sleepover Club, Animal Ark, Dolphin Diaries, Beast Quest, Naughty Fairies, Dream Dogs, Animal Antics, Scarlet Silver, Wild, and Space Penguins. Additionally, her desk drawers are filled with half-finished stories waiting for the right moment to emerge and dance around. In her spare time, she sings with assorted choirs and forages for mushrooms (which her husband wisely refuses to eat).

ABOUT THE ILLUSTRATOR

JAMES DAVIES is a London-based illustrator, author, and pro-wrestling expert who grew up in the 1980s and loved to draw video--game bad guys and dig in the garden for dinosaur bones. Since then, James has gone to college, gotten a haircut or two, and is extremely busy working on all kinds of book projects.

GLOSSARY

BANISTER (BAN-is-ter)—the handrail that runs along a staircase

BOAST (BOHST)—to brag or talk about something in order to impress others

COORDINATES (koh-OR-duh-nits)—a set of numbers that tells the position of a specific place

FUSELAGE (FYOO-suh-lahzh)—the main part of an aircraft that holds the passengers, crew, and cargo

METEOR (MEE-tee-ur)—a piece of rock or metal that falls into a planet's atmosphere and creates a streak of light as it burns up

MINE (MAHYN)—a hidden bomb that goes off when touched

PENNANT (PEN-uhnt)—a long flag shaped like a triangle

SLOP (SLAHP)—food scraps that are eaten by animals, especially pigs

SOLDER (SAH-der)—to join two pieces of metal by using melted metal

SPECTATOR (SPEK-tay-ter)—a person that only watches an event

TAMPER (TAM-pur)—to secretly damage something so that it no longer works

TANTRUM (TAN-truhm)—a sudden outburst of anger

DISCUSSION QUESTIONS

1. Why do you think Anadin Skyporker always cheated in the races? Have you ever been in a competition where someone didn't follow the rules?

2. The Space Penguins work best as a team. Talk about a time when you worked in a team. Was it better than doing everything by yourself?

3. Why do you think Rocky didn't listen to the other penguins when they warned him about the race? Discuss some possible reasons.

WRITING PROMPTS

1. Imagine you were one of the racers entered in the Superchase Space Race. Describe your ship and write a story about how you did in the race.

2. Argos Megabux thought his ship was useless because it smelled bad, but the Space Penguins thought it was the best ship in the universe. Write about an object that you think is very useful, but someone else might think is trash.

3. Think of a time when you did well in a competition. How did you feel afterward?